Utah, Tribune Job Printing Company

Constitution of the State of Utah

As framed by the Constitutional Convention in Salt Lake City, Utah, from

March 4th, to May 8th, 1895

Utah, Tribune Job Printing Company

Constitution of the State of Utah
As framed by the Constitutional Convention in Salt Lake City, Utah, from March 4th,
to May 8th, 1895

ISBN/EAN: 9783337406219

Printed in Europe, USA, Canada, Australia, Japan

Cover: Foto ©Andreas Hilbeck / pixelio.de

More available books at **www.hansebooks.com**

CONSTITUTION

OF THE

STATE OF UTAH

AS FRAMED BY THE

CONSTITUTIONAL CONVENTION

IN

SALT LAKE CITY, UTAH,

From March 4th, to May 8th, 1895.

Published by Authority of the Convention
under the Supervision of

HON. RICHARD G. LAMBERT,

Chairman of Committee on Printing.

SALT LAKE CITY:
TRIBUNE JOB PRINTING COMPANY.

1895.

NAME WAS GIVEN TO UTAH BY FIRST EXPLORER, PRIEST

Father Escalante Started to Blaze

Trail From Santa Fe to

California Missions

(From the Salt Lake Tribune)

Fray Silvestre Velez de Escalante, Fray Francisco Atanasio Dominguez and seven others—men-at-arms, guides and civilians—started yesterday morning from the Franciscan mission at Santa Fe to blaze a trail to Monterey and the California missions. Last night the party had completed nine leagues and camped at Santa Clara.

But all this was 150 years ago—July 29, 1776—when the history of Utah, in so far as the mind of man is concerned was unmade.

Father Escalante's famous journey was the discovery of Utah, and the first use of the word "Utah" in the history of man was made by the intrepid priest-explorer in his lucid description of his journey northward as far as the shores of the present Utah Lake. He adopted the Indian name both for Utah Valley and for its guardian sentinel, Mount Timpanogos, when he named the Utah Lake region "the valley and lake of Our Lady of Mercy of Timpagtiz, or Timpanogotzis." Mount Timpanogos was thought to be a peak of the Sierras then.

After reaching the shores of Utah Lake Sept. 23, 1776, the party learned of Great Salt Lake, described by the Indians as "very harmful and very salty." Father Escalante did not go to the shores of Great Salt Lake, but abandoned his search for a new trail to California and turned southward. The route of the party on the return to Sante Fe included Southern Utah's wonderland, the site of Cedar City and the Rio Virgin.

Father Escalante's famous trip to Utah was completed Jan. 2, 1777, when the party reached Sante Fe. His **journal**, now preserved in the royal **archives** of Spain at Seville, **details the climate of** the country of the "Utahs," **the general** name **of the** Indian **tribes, and the** possibilities **for** future development.

WHERE TRAINED MEN ARE

HON. RICHARD G. LAMBERT.

LAMBERT PAPER CO:,
23 WEST FIRST SOUTH STREET,
SALT LAKE CITY.

To the People of Utah:

The Convention assembled to frame a Constitution for the proposed State of Utah, after two months of earnest effort, present the result of their labors for the consideration of the people of this Territory.

The ruling thought that actuated the Convention, from opening to close, was that under the direction and mandates of the Enabling Act, a Constitution must be framed that would secure to the people of Utah a wise, just and economical State government.

In this we believe we have succeeded, and we confidently submit to our fellow citizens the fruit of our deliberations, knowing that they will bear in mind the impossibility of our presenting any instrument that would not contain imperfections, inasmuch as the more than one hundred delegates who constructed it came together understanding little of each other, all more or less influenced by local ideas, and by impressions which the peculiar situation of this Territory for years past could not help but create and intensify. Nevertheless, it has been gratifying to note that there has been less partisan feeling and more unselfish unanimity of sentiment in this Convention than in any other political body of like character.

The inspiration behind the Declaration of Rights came from the great parent Bill of Rights framed by the Fathers of our country.

The article on the proposed Educational System has absorbed the best thoughts and efforts of the Convention, and draws around the Public Schools such protection and defense as will secure for them, it is believed, the steady upward progress which is the enthusiastic desire of this people.

The Legislative Article, while permitting future law-makers to perform any needed thing, circumscribes their powers in a way to prevent either extravagance or the misuse of legislative authority.

The Executive Article defines clearly the prerogatives and powers of the several State officers, places all necessary authority in the hands of the Executive, and at the same time supplies all needed checks to prevent usurpation of power.

The Judiciary Article makes possible the conducting of the courts effectively by competent judges. It seeks to exalt the judiciary, and yet brings the system within a reasonable expenditure of the people's money. The Probate System has been abolished, but power is given the Legislature to restore it, if deemed necessary, or to adopt any other plan that may be wise or expedient.

The salaries of all officials have been marked down close to the danger line of extravagant economy.

We have provided to give equal suffrage to women.

We have inhibited for all time polygamous or plural marriages.

We have placed within safe limits the maximum of future taxation.

We have guarded against the possibility of any future great indebtedness of the State.

We have provided for the full development of our manifold industries, in such a way that in their expansion they will not feel any harsh friction from unjust laws.

We have provided for the correction of possible defects in the Constitution, either by amendments or by the enactment of statutes.

We have guaranteed perfect liberty of speech, freedom to the press, and absolute freedom of conscience.

We recommend our work to the gracious and generous consideration of the men and women of Utah, believing they will esteem it a fitting foundation on which to rear the structure of a glorified State.

If with Statehood there will be a slight increase in taxes, the compensating advantages will cause the increased expense to be forgotten. We will be able to utilize the magnificent gift of over seven millions of acres of land from our generous government; we will be able to secure capital for our mines; under the shield of Statehood thousands of people will seek homes in our climate, assist to develop our wondrous and varied resources, and rejoice in the manifold blessings bestowed by nature upon our highly favored commonwealth.

When we reflect that this instrument will secure to us in its highest sense local self-government, with State officers of our own selection, and courts for the swift, capable and economical administration of the laws by judges of the people's choosing; that it will give us a school system abreast of the foremost in the Union, with power to utilize the lands donated to our educational institutions; give us a voice in the election of Presidents, also two Senators and one Representative to present the claims of our new State in the Congress of the Nation; add the Star of Utah to the hallowed ensign of the Republic, bestow upon us full sovereignty, with all that this majestic term implies, and thus draw to us capital and population, and invest us with a dignity that can never attach to a Territorial condition, with steadily swelling confidence we submit this Constitution to the consideration of the people of Utah, in a certain belief that they will, by an overwhelming majority endorse and ratify our work.

CONTENTS.

PREAMBLE.

Grateful to Almighty God for life and liberty, we, the people of Utah, in order to secure and perpetuate the principles of free government, do ordain and establish this

CONSTITUTION.

ARTICLE I.

DECLARATION OF RIGHTS.

SECTION 1. All men have the inherent and inalienable right to enjoy and defend their lives and liberties; to acquire, possess and protect property; to worship according to the dictates of their consciences; to assemble peaceably, protest against wrongs, and petition for redress of grievances; to communicate freely their thoughts and opinions, being responsible for the abuse of that right.

SEC. 2. All political power is inherent in the people; and all free governments are founded on their authority for their equal protection and benefit, and they have the right to alter or reform their government as the public welfare may require.

SEC. 3. The State of Utah is an inseparable part of the Federal Union, and the Constitution of the United States is the supreme law of the land.

SEC. 4. The rights of conscience shall never be infringed. The State shall make no law respecting an establishment of religion or prohibiting the free exercise thereof; no religious test shall be required as a qualification for any office of public trust or for any vote at any election; nor shall any person be incompetent as a witness or juror on account of religious belief or the absence thereof. There shall be no union of church and State, nor shall any church dominate the State or interfere with its functions. No public money or property shall be appropriated for or applied to any religious worship, exercise or instruction, or for the support of any ecclesiastical establishment. No property qualication shall be required of any person to vote, or hold office, except as provided in this Constitution.

SEC. 5. The privilege of the writ of *habeas corpus* shall not be suspended, unless, in case of rebellion or invasion, the public safety requires it.

SEC. 6. The people have the right to bear arms for their security and defense, but the Legislature may regulate the exercise of this right by law.

SEC. 7. No person shall be deprived of life, liberty or property, without due process of law.

SEC. 8. All prisoners shall be bailable by sufficient sureties, except for capital offenses when the proof is evident or the presumption strong.

SEC. 9. Excessive bail shall not be required; excessive fines shall not be imposed; nor shall cruel and unusual punishments be inflicted. Persons arrested or imprisoned shall not be treated with unnecessary rigor.

SEC. 10. In capital cases the right of trial by jury shall remain inviolate. In courts of general jurisdiction, except in capital cases, a jury shall consist of eight jurors. In courts of inferior jurisdiction a jury shall consist of four jurors. In criminal cases the verdict shall be unanimous. In civil cases three-fourths of the jurors may find a verdict. A jury in civil cases shall be waived unless demanded.

SEC. 11. All courts shall be open, and every person, for an injury done to him in his person, property or reputation, shall have remedy by due course of law, which shall be administered without denial or unnecessary delay; and no person shall be barred from prosecuting or defending before any tribunal in this State, by himself or counsel, any civil cause to which he is a party.

SEC. 12. In criminal prosecutions the accused shall have the right to appear and defend in person and by counsel, to demand the nature and cause of the accusation against him, to have a copy thereof, to testify in his own behalf, to be confronted by the witnesses against him, to have compulsory process to compel the attendance of witnesses in his own behalf, to have a speedy public trial by an impartial jury of the county or district in which the offense is alleged to have been committed, and the right to appeal in all cases. In no instance shall any accused person, before final judgment, be compelled to advance money or fees to secure the rights herein guaranteed. The accused shall not be compelled to give evidence against himself; a wife shall not be compelled to testify against her husband, nor a husband against his wife, nor shall any person be twice put in jeopardy for the same offense.

SEC. 13. Offenses heretofore required to be prosecuted by indictment, shall be prosecuted by information after examination and commitment by a magistrate, unless the examination be waived by the accused with the consent of the State, or by indictment, with or without such examination and commitment. The grand jury shall consist of seven persons, five of whom must concur to find an indictment; but no grand jury shall be drawn or summoned unless in the opinion of the judge of the district, public interest demands it.

SEC. 14. The right of the people to be secure in their persons, houses, papers and effects against unreasonable searches and seizures shall not be violated; and no warrant shall issue but upon probable cause supported by oath or affirmation, particularly describing the place to be searched and the person or thing to be seized.

SEC. 15. No law shall be passed to abridge or restrain the freedom of speech or of the press. In all criminal prosecutions for libel the truth may be given in evidence to the jury; and if it shall appear to the jury that the matter charged as libelous is true, and was published with good motives, and for justifiable ends, the party shall be acquitted; and the jury shall have the right to determine the law and the fact.

SEC. 16. There shall be no imprisonment for debt, except in cases of absconding debtors.

SEC. 17. All elections shall be free, and no power, civil or military, shall at any time interfere to prevent the free exercise of the right of suffrage. Soldiers in time of war, may vote at their post of duty, in or out of the State, under regulations to be prescribed by law.

SEC. 18. No bill of attainder, *ex post facto* law, or law impairing the obligation of contracts shall be passed.

Sec. 19. Treason against the State shall consist only in levying war against it, or in adhering to its enemies or in giving them aid and comfort. No person shall be convicted of treason unless on the testimony of two witnesses to the same overt act.

Sec. 20. The military shall be in strict subordination to the civil power, and no soldier in time of peace, shall be quartered in any house without the consent of the owner; nor in time of war except in a manner to be prescribed by law.

Sec. 21. Neither slavery nor involuntary servitude, except as a punishment for crime, whereof the party shall have been duly convicted, shall exist within this State.

Sec. 22. Private property shall not be taken or damaged for public use without just compensation.

Sec. 23. No law shall be passed granting irrevocably any franchise, privilege or immunity.

Sec. 24. All laws of a general nature shall have uniform operation.

Sec. 25. This enumeration of rights shall not be construed to impair or deny others retained by the people.

Sec. 26. The provisions of this Constitution are mandatory and prohibitory, unless by express words they are declared to be otherwise.

Sec. 27. Frequent recurrence to fundamental principles is essential to the security of individual rights and the perpetuity of free government.

ARTICLE II.

STATE BOUNDARIES.

Section 1. The boundaries of the State of Utah shall be as follows:

Beginning at a point formed by the intersection of the thirty-second degree of longitude west from Washington, with the thirty-seventh degree of north latitude; thence due west along said thirty-seventh degree of north latitude to the intersection of the same with the thirty-seventh degree of longitude west from Washington; thence due north along said thirty-

seventh degree of west longitude to the intersection of the same
with the forty-second degree of north latitude; thence due east
along said forty-second degree of north latitude to the intersection of the same with the thirty-fourth degree of longitude west
from Washington; thence due south along said thirty-fourth
degree of west longitude to the intersection of the same with
the forty-first degree of north latitude; thence due east along
said forty-first degree of north latitude to the intersection of
the same with the thirty-second degree of longitude west from
Washington; thence due south along said thirty-second degree
of west longitude to the place of beginning.

ARTICLE III

ORDINANCE.

The following ordinance shall be irrevocable without the
consent of the United States and the people of this State:

First:—Perfect toleration of religious sentiment is guaranteed. No inhabitant of this State shall ever be molested in
person or property on account of his or her mode of religious
worship; but polygamous or plural marriages are forever prohibited.

Second:—The people inhabiting this State do affirm and
declare that they forever disclaim all right and title to the
unappropriated public lands lying within the boundaries hereof,
and to all lands lying within said limits owned or held by any
Indian or Indian tribes, and that until the title thereto shall
have been extinguished by the United States, the same shall be
and remain subject to the disposition of the United States, and
said Indian lands shall remain under the absolute jurisdiction
and control of the Congress of the United States. The lands
belonging to citizens of the United States, residing without this
State shall never be taxed at a higher rate than the lands
belonging to residents of this State; nor shall taxes be imposed
by this State on lands or property herein, belonging to or which
may hereafter be purchased by the United States or reserved
for its use; but nothing in this ordinance shall preclude this
State from taxing, as other lands are taxed, any lands owned or

held by any Indian who has severed his tribal relations, and
has obtained from the United States or from any person, by
patent or other grant, a title thereto, save and except such land
as have been or may be granted to any Indian or Indians unde
any act of Congress, containing a provision exempting the land
thus granted from taxation, which last mentioned lands shal
be exempt from taxation so long, and to such extent, as is o
may be provided in the act of Congress granting the same.

Third:—All debts and liabilities of the Territory of Utah,
incurred by authority of the Legislative Assembly thereof, are
hereby assumed and shall be paid by this State.

Fourth:—The legislature shall make laws for the establishment and maintenance of a system of public schools, which
shall be open to all the children of the State and be free from
sectarian control.

ARTICLE IV.

ELECTIONS AND RIGHT OF SUFFRAGE.

SECTION 1. The rights of citizens of the State of Utah to
vote and hold office snall not be denied or abridged on account
of sex. Both male and female citizens of this State shall enjoy
equally all civil, political and religious rights and privileges.

SEC. 2. Every citizen of the United States, of the age of
twenty-one years and upwards, who shall have been a citizen
for ninety days, and shall have resided in the State or Territory
one year, in the county four months, and in the precinct sixty
days next preceding any election, shall be entitled to vote at
such election except as herein otherwise provided.

SEC. 3. In all cases except those of treason, felony or
breach of the peace, electors shall be privileged from arrest on
the days of election, during their attendance at elections, and
going to and returning therefrom.

SEC. 4. No elector shall be obliged to perform militia
duty on the day of election except in time of war or public
danger.

SEC. 5. No person shall be deemed a qualified elector of
this State unless such person be a citizen of the United States.

Sec. 6. No idiot, insane person or person convicted of treason, or crime against the elective franchise, unless restored to civil rights, shall be permitted to vote at any election, or be eligible to hold office in this State.

Sec. 7. Except in elections levying a special tax or creating indebtedness, no property qualification shall be required for any person to vote or hold office.

Sec. 8. All elections shall be by secret ballot. Nothing in this section shall be construed to prevent the use of any machine or mechanical contrivance for the purpose of receiving and registering the votes cast at any election: *Provided*, That secrecy in voting be preserved.

Sec. 9. All general elections, except for municipal and school officers, shall be held on the Tuesday next following the first Monday in November of the year in which the election is held. Special elections may be held as provided by law. The terms of all officers elected at any general election shall commence on the first Monday in January next following the date of their election. Municipal and school officers shall be elected at such time as may be provided by law.

Sec. 10. All officers made elective or appointive by this Constitution or by the laws made in pursuance thereof, before entering upon the duties of their respective offices, shall take and subscribe the following oath or affirmation: "I do solemnly swear (or affirm) that I will support, obey and defend the Constitution of the United States and the Constitution of this State, and that I will discharge the duties of my office with fidelity."

ARTICLE V.

DISTRIBUTION OF POWERS.

Section 1. The powers of the government of the State of Utah shall be divided into three distinct departments, the Legislative, the Executive, and the Judicial; and no person charged with the exercise of powers properly belonging to one of these departments, shall exercise any functions appertaining to either of the others, except in the cases herein expressly directed or permitted.

ARTICLE VI.

LEGISLATIVE DEPARTMENT.

SECTION 1. The Legislative power of this State shall be vested in a Senate and House of Representatives, which shall be designated The Legislature of the State of Utah.

SEC. 2. Regular sessions of the Legislature shall be held biennially at the seat of the government; and except the first session thereof shall commence on the second Monday in January next after the election of members of the House of Representatives.

SEC. 3. The members of the House of Representatives, after the first election, shall be chosen by the qualified electors of the respective representative districts, on the first Tuesday after the first Monday in November, 1896, and biennially thereafter. Their term of office shall be two years, from the first day of January next after their election.

SEC. 4. The senators shall be chosen by the qualified electors of the respective senatorial districts, at the same times and places as members of the House of Representatives, and their term of office shall be four years from the first day of January next after their election: *Provided*, That the senators elected in 1896 shall be divided by lot into two classes as nearly equal as may be; seats of senators of the first class shall be vacated at the expiration of two years, those of the second class at the expiration of four years; so that one-half, as near as possible, shall be chosen biennially thereafter. In case of increase in the number of senators, they shall be annexed by lot to one or the other of the two classes, so as to keep them as nearly equal as practicable.

SEC. 5. No person shall be eligible to the office of senator or representative, who is not a citizen of the United States, twenty-five years of age, a qualified voter in the district from which he is chosen, a resident for three years of the State, and for one year of the district from which he is elected.

SEC. 6. No person holding any public office of profit or trust under authority of the United States, or of this State, shall be a member of the Legislature: *Provided*, That appointments in the State militia, and the offices of notary public, justice of the peace, United States commissioner, and postmaster of the fourth class, shall not, within the meaning of this section, be considered offices of profit or trust.

SEC. 7. No member of tho Legislature, during the term for which he was elected, shall be appointed or elected to any civil office of profit under this State, which shall have been created, or the emoluments of which shall have been increased, during the term for which he was elected.

SEC. 8. Members of the Legislature, in all cases except treason, felony or breach of peace, shall be privileged from arrest during each session of the Legislature, for fifteen days next preceding each session, and in returning therefrom; and for words used in any speech or debate in either house, they shall not be questioned in any other place.

SEC. 9. The members of the Legislature shall receive such per diem and mileage as the Legislature may provide, not exceeding four dollars per day, and ten cents per mile for the distance necessarily traveled going to and returning from the place of meeting on the most usual route, and they shall receive no other pay or perquisite.

SEC. 10. Each house shall be the judge of the election and qualifications of its members, and may punish them for disorderly conduct, and with the concurrence of two-thirds of all the members elected, expel a member for cause.

SEC. 11. A majority of the members of each house shall constitute a quorum to transact business, but a smaller number may adjourn from day to day, and may compel the attendance of absent members in such manner and under such penalties as each house may prescribe.

SEC. 12. Each house shall determine the rules of its proceedings, and choose its own officers and employees.

SEC. 13. The Governor shall issue writs of election to fill vacancies that may occur in either house of the Legislature.

SEC. 14. Each house shall keep a journal of its proceedings, which, except in case of executive sessions, shall be published, and the yeas and nays on any question, at the request of five members of such house, shall be entered upon the journal.

SEC. 15. All sessions of the Legislature, except those of the Senate while sitting in executive session, shall be public; and neither house, without the consent of the other, shall adjourn for more than three days, nor to any other place than that in which it may be holding session.

SEC. 16. No regular session of the Legislature (except the first, which may sit ninety days) shall exceed sixty days, except in cases of impeachment. No special session shall exceed thirty days, and in such special session, or when a regular session of the Legislature trying cases of impeachment exceeds sixty days, the members shall receive for compensation only the usual per diem and mileage.

SEC. 17. The House of Representatives shall have the sole power of impeachment, but in order to impeach, two-thirds of all the members elected must vote therefor.

SEC. 18. All impeachments shall be tried by the Senate, and senators, when sitting for that purpose, shall take oath or make affirmation to do justice according to the law and the evidence. When the Governor is on trial, the Chief Justice of the Supreme Court shall preside. No person shall be convicted without the concurrence of two-thirds of the Senators elected.

SEC. 19. The Governor and other State and Judicial officers, except justices of the peace, shall be liable to impeachment for high crimes, misdemeanors, or malfeasance in office; but judgment in such cases shall extend only to removal from office and disqualification to hold any office of honor, trust or profit in the State. The party, whether convicted or acquitted, shall, nevertheless, be liable to prosecution, trial and punishment according to law.

SEC. 20. No person shall be tried on impeachment, unless he shall have been served with a copy of the articles thereof, at least ten days before the trial, and after such service he shall not exercise the duties of his office until he shall have been acquitted.

SEC. 21. All officers not liable to impeachment shall be removed for any of the offenses specified in this article, in such manner as may be provided by law.

SEC. 22. The enacting clause of every law shall be: "Be it enacted by the Legislature of the State of Utah," and no bill or joint resolution shall be passed, except with the assent of a majority of all the members elected to each house of the Legislature, and after it has been read three times. The vote upon the final passage of all bills shall be by yeas and nays; and no law shall be revised or amended by reference to its title only; but the act as revised, or section as amended, shall be re-enacted and published at length.

SEC. 23. Except general appropriation bills, and bills for the codification and general revision of laws, no bill shall be passed containing more than one subject, which shall be clearly expressed in its title.

SEC. 24. The presiding officer of each house, in the presence of the house over which he presides, shall sign all bills and joint resolutions passed by the Legislature, after their titles have been publicly read immediately before signing, and the fact of such signing shall be entered upon the journal.

SEC. 25. All acts shall be officially published, and no act shall take effect until so published, nor until sixty days after the adjournment of the session at which it passed, unless the Legislature by vote of two-thirds of all the members elected to each house, shall otherwise direct.

SEC. 26. The Legislature is prohibited from enacting any private or special laws in the following cases:

First.—Granting divorce.

Second.—Changing the names of persons or places, or constituting one person the heir at law of another.

Third.—Locating or changing county seats.

Fourth.—Regulating the jurisdiction and duties of justices of the peace.

Fifth.—Punishing crimes and misdemeanors.

Sixth.—Regulating the practice of courts of justice.

Seventh.—Providing for a change of venue in civil or criminal actions.

Eighth.—Assessing and collecting taxes.

Ninth.—Regulating the interest on money.

Tenth.—Changing the law of descent or succession.

Eleventh.—Regulating county and township affairs.

Twelfth.—Incorporating cities, towns or villages; changing or amending the charter of any city, town or village; laying out, opening, vacating or altering town plats, highways, streets, wards, alleys or public grounds.

Thirteenth.—Providing for sale or mortgage of real estate belonging to minors or others under disability.

Fourteenth.—Authorizing persons to keep ferries across streams within the State.

Fifteenth.—Remitting fines, penalties or forfeitures.

Sixteenth.—Granting to an individual, association or corporation any privilege, immunity or franchise.

Seventeenth.—Providing for the management of common schools.

Eighteenth.—Creating, increasing or decreasing fees, percentages or allowances of public officers during the term for which said officers are elected or appointed.

The Legislature may repeal any existing special law relating to the foregoing subdivisions.

In all cases where a general law can be applicable, no special law shall be enacted.

Nothing in this section shall be construed to deny or restrict the power of the Legislature to establish and regulate the compensation and fees of county and township officers; to establish and regulate the rates of freight, passage, toll and charges of railroads, toll roads, ditch, flume and tunnel companies, incorporated under the laws of the State or doing business therein.

SEC. 27. The Legislature shall have no power to release or extinguish, in whole or in part, the indebtedness, liability or obligation of any corporation or person to the State, or to any municipal corporation therein.

SEC. 28. The Legislature shall not authorize any game of chance, lottery or gift enterprise under any pretense or for any purpose.

SEC. 29. The Legislature shall not delegate to any special commission, private corporation or association, any power to make, supervise or interfere with any municipal improvement, money, property or effects, whether held in trust or otherwise, to levy taxes, to select a capitol site, or to perform any municipal functions.

SEC. 30. The Legislature shall have no power to grant, or authorize any county or municipal authority to grant, any extra compensation, fee or allowance to any public officer, agent, servant or contractor, after service has been rendered or a contract has been entered into and performed in whole or in part, nor pay or authorize the payment of any claim hereafter created against the State, or any county or municipality of the State, under any agreement or contract made without authority of law: Provided, That this section shall not apply to claims incurred by public officers in the execution of the laws of the State.

SEC. 31. The Legislature shall not authorize the State, or any county, city, town, township, district or other political subdivision of the State to lend its credit or subscribe to stock or bonds in aid of any railroad, telegraph or other private individual or corporate enterprise or undertaking.

ARTICLE VII.

EXECUTIVE.

SECTION 1. The Executive Department shall consist of Governor, Secretary of State, State Auditor, State Treasurer, Attorney-General, and Superintendent of Public Instruction, each of whom shall hold his office for four years, beginning on the first Monday of January next after his election, except that the terms of office of those elected at the first election shall begin when the State shall be admitted into the Union, and shall end on the first Monday in January, A. D. 1901. The officers of the Executive Department, during their terms of office, shall reside at the seat of government, where they shall keep the public records, books and papers. They shall perform such duties as are prescribed by this Constitution and as may be prescribed by law.

SEC. 2. The officers provided for in section one of this article, shall be elected by the qualified electors of the State at the time and place of voting for members of the Legislature, and the persons respectively having the highest number of votes cast for the office voted for shall be elected; but if two or more shall have an equal and highest number of votes for any one of said offices, the two houses of the Legislature, at its next regular session, shall elect forthwith by joint ballot one of such persons for said office.

SEC. 3. No person shall be eligible to the office of Governor or Secretary of State unless he shall have attained the age of thirty years at the time of his election, nor to the office of Attorney-General unless he shall have attained the age of twenty-five years at the time of his election, and have been admitted to practice in the Supreme Court of the Territory or of the State of Utah, nor unless he shall be in good standing at the bar at the time of his election. No person shall be eligible to any of the offices provided for in section one of this article, unless at the time of his election he shall be a qualified elector, and shall have been a resident citizen of the State or Territory for five years next preceding his election. The State Auditor and State Treasurer shall be ineligible to election as their own successors.

SEC. 4. The Governor shall be commander-in-chief of the military forces of the State, except when they shall be called into the service of the United States. He shall have the power to call out the militia to execute the laws, to suppress insurrection, or to repel invasion.

SEC. 5. The Governor shall see that the laws are faithfully executed; he shall transact all executive business with the officers of the government, civil and military, and may require information in writing from the officers of the Executive Department, and from the officers and managers of State Institutions upon any subject relating to the condition, management, and expenses of their respective offices and institutions, and at any time when the Legislative Assembly is not in session, may, if he deem it necessary, appoint a committee to investigate and report to him upon the condition of any executive office or State institution. He shall communicate by message the condition of the State to the Legislature at every regular session, and recommend such measures as he may deem expedient.

SEC. 6. On extraordinary occasions, the Governor may convene the Legislature by proclamation, in which shall be stated the purpose for which the Legislature is to be convened, and it shall transact no legislative business except that for which it was especially convened, or such other legislative business as the Governor may call to its attention while in session. The Legislature, however, may provide for the expenses of the session and other matters incidental thereto. The Governor may also by proclamation convene the Senate in extraordinary session for the transaction of executive business.

SEC. 7. In case of a disagreement between the two houses of the Legislature at any special session, with respect to the time of adjournment, the Governor shall have power to adjourn the Legislature to such time as he may think proper: *Provided*, it be not beyond the time fixed for the convening of the next Legislature.

SEC. 8. Every bill passed by the Legislature, before it becomes a law, shall be presented to the Governor; if he approve, he shall sign it, and thereupon it shall become a law; but if he do not approve, he shall return it with his objections to the house in which it originated, which house shall enter the objections at large upon its journal and proceed to reconsider the bill. If, after such reconsideration, it again passes both houses by a yea and nay vote of two-thirds of the members elected to each house, it shall become a law, notwithstanding the Governor's objections. If any bill be not returned within five days after it shall have been presented to him (Sunday and the day on which he received it excepted), the same shall be a law in like manner as if he had signed it, unless the Legislature by its final adjournment prevent such return, in which case it shall be filed with his objections in the office of the Secretary of State within ten days after such adjournment (Sundays excepted) or become a law. If any bill presented to the Governor contains several items of appropriations of money, he may object to one or more such items, while approving other portions of the bill; in such case he shall append to the bill at the time of signing it a statement of the item or items which he declines to approve, together with his reasons therefor, and such item or items shall not take effect unless passed over the Governor's objection as in this section provided.

SEC. 9. When any State or district office shall become vacant, and no mode is provided by the Constitution and laws for filling such vacancy, the Governor shall have the power to fill the same by granting a commission, which shall expire at the next election, and upon qualification of the person elected to such office.

SEC. 10. The Governor shall nominate, and by and with the consent of the Senate, appoint all State and district officers whose offices are established by this Constitution, or which may be created by law, and whose appointment or election is not otherwise provided for. If, during the recess of the Senate, a vacancy occur in any State or district office, the Governor shall appoint some fit person to discharge the duties thereof until the next meeting of the Senate, when he shall nominate some person to fill such office. If the office of Justice of the Supreme or District Court, Secretary of State, State Auditor, State Treasurer, Attorney-General or Superintendent of Public Instruction be vacated by death, resignation or otherwise, it shall be the duty of the Governor to fill the same by appointment, and the appointee shall hold his office until his successor shall be elected and qualified, as may be by law provided.

SEC. 11. In case of the death of the Governor, or his impeachment, removal from office, inability to discharge the duties of his office, resignation or absence from the State, the powers and duties of said office shall devolve upon the Secretary of State, until the disability shall cease, or until the next general election, when the vacancy shall be filled by election. If, during a vacancy in the office of the Governor, the Secretary of State resign, die or become incapable of performing the duties of the office, or bo displaced, or be absent from the State, the President *pro tempore* of the Senate shall act as Governor until the vacancy be filled or the disability cease. While performing the duties of the Governor as in this section provided, the Secretary of State, or the President *pro tempore* of the Senate, as the case may be, except in cases of temporary disability, or absence from the State, shall be entitled to the salary and emoluments of the Governor.

SEC. 12. Until otherwise provided by law, the Governor, Justices of the Supreme Court and Attorney-General shall constitute a Board of Pardons, a majority of whom, including the Governor, upon such conditions, and with such limitations and restrictions as they deem proper, may remit fines and forfeitures, commute punishments, and grant pardons after convictions, in all cases except treason and impeachments, subject to such regulations as may be provided by law, relative to the manner of applying for pardons; but no fine or forfeiture shall bo remitted, and no commutation or pardon granted, except after a full hearing before the Board, in open session, after previous notice of the time and place of such hearing has been given. The proceedings and decisions of the Board, with the reasons therefor in each case, together with the dissent of any member who may disagree, shall be reduced to writing, and filed with all papers used upon the hearing, in the office of the Secretary of State.

The Governor shall have power to grant respites or reprieves in all cases of convictions for offenses against the State, except treason or conviction on impeachment; but such respites or reprieves shall not extend beyond the next session of the Board of Pardons; and such Board, at such session, shall continue or determine such respite or reprieve, or they may commute the punishment, or pardon the offense as herein provided. In case of conviction for treason, the Governor shall have the power to suspend execution of the sentence, until the case shall be reported to the Legislature at its next regular session, when the Legislature shall either pardon, or commute the sentence, or direct its execution; he shall communicate to the Legislature at each regular session, each case of remission of fine or forfeiture, reprieve, commutation or pardon granted since the last previous report, stating the name of the convict, the crime for which he was convicted, the sentence and its date, the date of remission, commutation, pardon or reprieve, with the reasons for granting the same, and the objections, if any, of any member of the Board made thereto.

SEC. 13. Until otherwise provided by law, the Governor, Secretary of State and Attorney-General shall constitute a Board of State Prison Commissioners, which board shall have such supervision of all matters connected with the State prison as may be provided by law. They shall, also, constitute a Board of Examiners, with power to examine all claims against the State except salaries or compensation of officers fixed by law, and perform such other duties as may be prescribed by law, and no other claim against the State, except for salaries and compensation of officers fixed by law, shall be passed upon by the Legislature without having been considered and acted upon by the said Board of Examiners.

SEC. 14. Until otherwise provided by law, the Governor, State Treasurer and State Auditor shall constitute a Board of Insane Asylum Commissioners. Said Board shall have such supervision of all matters connected with the State Insane Asylum as may be provided by law.

SEC. 15. Until otherwise provided by law, the Governor, Attorney-General and Superintendent of Public Instruction shall constitute a Board of Reform School Commissioners. Said board shall have such supervision of all matters connected with the State Reform School as may be provided by law.

SEC. 16. The Secretary of State shall keep a record of the official acts of the Legislature and Executive Department of the State, and, when required, shall lay the same and all matters relative thereto before either branch of the Legislature, and shall perform such other duties as may be provided by law.

SEC. 17. The Auditor shall be Auditor of Public Accounts, and the Treasurer shall be the custodian of public moneys, and each shall perform such other duties as may be provided by law.

SEC. 18. The Attorney-General shall be the legal adviser of the State officers, and shall perform such other duties as may be provided by law.

SEC. 19. The Superintendent of Public Instruction shall perform such duties as may be provided by law.

SEC. 20. The Governor, Secretary of State, Auditor, Treasurer, Attorney-General, Superintendent of Public Instruction and such other State and district officers as may be provided for by law, shall receive for their services quarterly, a compensation as fixed by law, which shall not be diminished or increased so as to affect the salary of any officer during his term, or the term next ensuing after the adoption of this Constitution, unless a vacancy occur, in which case the successor of the former incumbent shall receive only such salary as may be provided by law at the time of his election or appointment. The compensation of the officers provided for by this article, until otherwise provided by law, is fixed as follows:

Governor, two thousand dollars per annum.

Secretary of State, two thousand dollars per annum.

State Auditor, fifteen hundred dollars per annum.

State Treasurer, one thousand dollars per annum.

Attorney-General, fifteen hundred dollars per annum.

Superintendent of Public Instruction, fifteen hundred dollars per annum.

The compensation for said officers as prescribed in this section, and in all laws enacted pursuant to this Constitution, shall be in full for all **services rendered** by said officers, respectively, **in any** official **capacity or** employment during their respective terms of office. No such officer shall receive **for the** performance of any official duty any fee for his own use, **but all** fees fixed by law for the performance by either of them of **any** official duty, shall be collected in advance **and** deposited **with the** State Treasurer quarterly to the credit of the State. The Legislature may provide **for** the payment **of** actual and **necessary** expenses of said officers while traveling in the State in the performance of official duty.

Sec. 21. All grants and commissions shall be in the name **and** by the authority **of** the State of Utah, sealed with the Great Seal **of** the State, signed by the Governor, and countersigned by **the** Secretary of **State.**

Sec. 22. There shall **be a seal of the State, which shall be** kept by **the** Secretary of **State, and** used by him officially. Said seal **shall be** called "The **Great Seal of the State of Utah."** The present seal of the Territory of Utah **shall be the seal of** the State until otherwise provided by law.

Sec. 23. No person, while holding any office under the United States government, shall hold any office under the State government **of** Utah, and **the** Governor shall not be eligible for election to the Senate of **the** United States during the term **for which he shall** have been elected Governor.

ARTICLE VIII.

JUDICIAL DEPARTMENT.

SECTION 1. The Judicial power **of the State** shall be vested **in the Senate** sitting as a court of **impeachment,** in a supreme court, in district courts, in justices **of the peace,** and such other **courts** inferior to the Supreme **Court as** may be established by law.

Sec. 2. The Supreme Court shall consist of three judges; but after the year A. D. 1905, the Legislature may increase the number thereof to five. A majority of the judges constituting the court **shall be necessary to** form a quorum or render a decision. If a justice of the Supreme Court shall be disqualified from sitting in a cause before said court, the remaining judges shall call a district judge to sit with them on the hearing of such cause. The Judges of the Supreme Court shall be elected by the electors of the State at large. The term of office of the Judges of the Supreme Court, excepting as in this article otherwise provided, shall be six years. The Judges of the Supreme Court, immediately after the first election under this Constitution, shall be selected by lot, so that one shall hold office for the term of three years, one for the term of five years, and one for the term of seven years. The lots shall be drawn by the Judges of the Supreme Court, who, for that purpose, shall assemble at the seat of government; and they shall cause the result thereof to be certified by the Secretary of State, and filed in his office. The judge having the shortest term to serve, not holding his office by appointment or election to fill a vacancy, shall be the Chief Justice, and shall preside at all terms of the Supreme Court, and in case of his absence, the judge, having in like manner, the next shortest term, shall preside in his stead.

Sec. 3. Every Judge of the Supreme Court shall be at least thirty years of age, and, before his election, shall be a member of the bar, learned in the law, and a resident of the Territory or State of Utah for five years next preceding his election.

Sec. 4. The Supreme Court shall have original jurisdiction to issue writs of *mandamus, certiorari*, prohibition, *quo-warranto* and *habeas corpus*. Each of the Justices shall have power to issue writs of *habeas corpus*, to any part of the State, upon petition by or on behalf of any person held in actual custody, and may make such writs returnable before himself or the Supreme Court, or before any district court or judge thereof in the State. In other cases the Supreme Court shall have appellate jurisdiction only, and power to issue writs necessary and proper for the exercise of that jurisdiction. The Supreme Court shall hold at least three terms every year, and shall sit at the capital of the State.

Sec. 5. The State shall be divided into seven judicial districts, for each of which, at least one, and not exceeding three judges, shall be chosen by the qualified electors thereof. The term of office of the district judges shall be four years, except that the district judges elected at the first election shall serve until the first Monday in January, A. D. 1901, and until their

successors shall have qualified.   Until otherwise provided by
law, a district court at the county seat of each county shall be
held at least four times a year.   All civil and criminal business
arising in any county, must be tried in such county, unless a
change of venue be taken, in such cases as may be provided by
law.   Each judge of the District Court shall be at least twenty-
five years of age, a member of the bar, learned in the law, a resident of the Territory or State of Utah three years next preceding his election, and shall reside in the district for which he
shall be elected.   Any District Judge may hold a District Court
in any county at the request of the judge of the district, and
upon a request of the Governor, it shall be his duty to do so.
Any cause in the District Court may be tried by a judge *pro
tempore*, who must be a member of the bar, sworn to try the
cause, and agreed upon by the parties, or their attorneys of
record.

Sec. 6.   The Legislature may change the limits of any
judicial district, or increase or decrease the number of districts,
or the judges thereof.   No alteration or increase shall have the
effect of removing a judge from office.   In every additional
district established, a judge shall be elected by the electors
thereof, and his term of office shall continue as provided in
section five of this article.

Sec. 7.   The District Court shall have original jurisdiction
in all matters civil and criminal, not excepted in this Constitution, and not prohibited by law; appellate jurisdiction from all
inferior courts and tribunals, and a supervisory control of the
same.   The District Courts or any judge thereof, shall have
power to issue writs of *habeas corpus, mandamus, injunction,
quo warranto, certiorari*, prohibition and other writs necessary
to carry into effect their orders, judgments and decrees, and to
give them a general control over inferior courts and tribunals
within their respective jurisdictions.

Sec. 8.   The Legislature shall determine the number of
justices of the peace to be elected, and shall fix by law their
powers, duties and compensation.   The jurisdiction of justices
of the peace shall be as now provided by law, but the Legislature may restrict the same.

Sec. 9.   From all final judgments of the District Courts,
there shall be a right of appeal to the Supreme Court.   The ap

peal shall be upon the record made in the court below, and under such regulations as may be provided by law. In equity cases the appeal may be on questions of both law and fact; in cases at law the appeal shall be on questions of law alone. Appeals shall also lie from the final orders and decrees of the Court in the administration of decedent estates, and in cases of guardianship, as shall be provided by law. Appeals shall also lie from the final judgment of justices of the peace in civil and criminal cases to the District Courts on both questions of law and fact, with such limitations and restrictions as shall be provided by law; and the decision of the District Courts on such appeals shall be final, except in cases involving the validity or constitutionality of a statute.

Sec. 10. A County Attorney shall be elected by the qualified voters of each county who shall hold his office for a term of two years. The powers and duties of County Attorneys and such other attorneys for the State as the Legislature may provide, shall be prescribed by law. In all cases where the attorney for any county, or for the State, fails or refuses to attend and prosecute according to law, the court shall have power to appoint an attorney *pro tempore.*

Sec. 11. Judges may be removed from office by the concurrent vote of both houses of the Legislature, each voting separately; but two-thirds of the members to which each house may be entitled must concur in such vote. The vote shall be determined by yeas and nays, and the names of the members voting for or against a judge, together with the cause or causes of removal, shall be entered on the journal of each house. The judge against whom the house may be about to proceed shall receive notice thereof, accompanied with a copy of the cause alleged for his removal, at least ten days before the day on which either house of the Legislature shall act thereon.

Sec. 12. The Judges of the Supreme and District Courts shall receive at stated times compensation for their services, which shall not be increased or diminished during the time for which they are elected.

Sec. 13. Except by consent of all the parties, no judge of the supreme or inferior courts shall preside in the trial of any cause where either of the parties shall be connected with him by affinity or consanguinity within the degree of first cousin, or in which he may have been of counsel, or in the trial of which he may have presided in any inferior court.

SEC. 14. The Supreme Court shall appoint a clerk, and a reporter of its decisions, who shall hold their offices during the pleasure of the Court. Until otherwise provided, County Clerks shall be *ex officio* clerks of the District Courts in and for their respective counties, and shall perform such other duties as may be provided by law.

SEC. 15. No person related to any judge of any court by affinity or consanguinity within the degree of first cousin, shall be appointed by such court or judge to, or employed by such court or judge in any office or duty in any court of which such judge may be a member.

SEC. 16. Until otherwise provided by law, the Judicial Districts of the State shall be constituted as follows:

First District: The Counties of Cache, Box Elder and Rich.

Second District: The Counties of Weber, Morgan and Davis.

Third District: The Counties of Summit, Salt Lake and Tooele, in which there shall be elected three district judges.

Fourth District: The Counties of Utah, Wasatch and Uintah.

Fifth District: The Counties of Juab, Millard, Beaver, Iron and Washington.

Sixth District: The Counties of Sevier, Piute, Wayne, Garfield and Kane.

Seventh District: The Counties of Sanpete, Carbon, Emery, Grand and San Juan.

SEC. 17. The Supreme and District courts shall be courts of record, and each shall have a seal.

SEC. 18. The style of all process shall be "The State of Utah," and all prosecutions shall be conducted in the name and by the authority of the same.

SEC. 19. There shall be but one form of civil action, and law and equity may be administered in the same action.

SEC. 20. Until otherwise provided by law, salaries of supreme and district judges, shall be three thousand dollars per annum and mileage, payable quarterly out of the State treasury.

Sec. 21. Judges of the Supreme Court, District Court, and justices of the peace, shall be conservators of the peace, and may hold preliminary examinations in cases of felony.

Sec. 22. District Judges may, at any time, report defects and omissions in the law to the Supreme Court, and the Supreme Court, on or before the first day of December of each year, shall report in writing to the Governor any seeming defect or omission in the law.

Sec. 23. The Legislature may provide for the publication of decisions and opinions of the Supreme Court, but all decisions shall be free to publishers.

Sec. 24. The terms of office of Supreme and District Judges may be extended by law, but such extension shall not affect the term for which any judge was elected.

Sec. 25. When a judgment or decree is reversed, modified or affirmed by the Supreme Court, the reasons therefor shall be stated concisely in writing, signed by the judges concurring, filed in the office of the Clerk of the Supreme Court, and preserved with a record of the case. Any judge dissenting therefrom, may give the reasons of his dissent in writing over his signature.

Sec. 26. It shall be the duty of the court to prepare a syllabus of all the points adjudicated in each case, which shall be concurred in by a majority of the judges thereof, and it shall be prefixed to the published reports of the case.

Sec. 27. Any judicial officer who shall absent himself from the State or district for more than ninety consecutive days, shall be deemed to have forfeited his office: *Provided,* That in case of extreme necessity, the Governor may extend the leave of absence to such time as the necessity therefor shall exist.

ARTICLE IX.

CONGRESSIONAL AND LEGISLATIVE APPORTIONMENT.

Section 1. One representative in the Congress of the United States shall be elected from the State at large on the Tuesday next after the first Monday in November, A. D. 1895, and thereafter at such times and places, and in such manner as may be prescribed by law. When a new apportionment shall be made by Congress, the Legislature shall divide the State into congressional districts accordingly.

SEC. 2. The Legislature shall provide by law for an enumeration of the inhabitants of the State, A. D. 1905, and every tenth year thereafter, and at the session next following such enumeration, and also at the session next following an enumeration made by the authority of the United States, shall revise and adjust the opportionment for Senators and Representatives on the basis of such enumeration according to ratios to be fixed by law.

SEC. 3. The Senate shall consist of eighteen members, and the House of Representatives of forty-five members. The Legislature may increase the number of Senators and Representatives, but the Senators shall never exceed thirty in number, and the number of Representatives shall never be less than twice nor greater than three times the number of Senators.

SEC. 4. When more than one county shall constitute a Senatorial District, such counties shall be contiguous, and no county shall be divided in the formation of such districts unless such county contains sufficient population within itself to form two or more districts, nor shall a part of any county be united with any other county in forming any district.

REPRESENTATIVE DISTRICTS.

Until otherwise provided by law, Representatives shall be apportioned among the several counties of the State as follows:

Provided, That in any future apportionment made by the Legislature, each county shall be entitled to at least one representative.

The County of Box Elder shall constitute the First Representative District, and be entitled to one representative.

The County of Cache shall constitute the Second Representative District, and be entitled to three representatives.

The County of Rich shall constitute the Third Representative District, and be entitled to one representative.

The County of Weber shall constitute the Fourth Representative District, and be entitled to four representatives.

The County of Morgan shall constitute the Fifth Representative District, and be entitled to one representative.

The County of Davis shall constitute the Sixth Representative District, and be entitled to one representative.

The County of Tooele shall constitute the Seventh Representative District, and be entitled to one representative.

The County of Salt Lake shall constitute the Eighth Representative District, and be entitled to ten representatives.

The County of Summit shall constitute the Ninth Representative District, and be entitled to one representative.

The County of Wasatch shall constitute the Tenth Representative District, and be entitled to one representative.

The County of Utah shall constitute the Eleventh Representative District, and be entitled to four representatives.

The County of Uintah shall constitute the Twelfth Representative District, and be entitled to one representative.

The County of Juab shall constitute the Thirteenth Representative District, and be entitled to one representative.

The County of Sanpete shall constitute the Fourteenth Representative District, and be entitled to two representatives.

The County of Carbon shall constitute the Fifteenth Representative District, and be entitled to one representative.

The County of Emery shall constitute the Sixteenth Representative District, and be entitled to one representative.

The County of Grand shall constitute the Seventeenth Representative District, and be entitled to one representative.

The County of Sevier shall constitute the Eighteenth Representative District, and be entitled to one representative.

The County of Millard shall constitute the Nineteenth Representative District, and be entitled to one representative.

The County of Beaver shall constitute the Twentieth Representative District, and be entitled to one representative.

The County of Piute shall constitute the Twenty-first Representative District, and be entitled to one representative.

The County of Wayne shall constitute the Twenty-second Representative District, and be entitled to one representative.

The County of Garfield shall constitute the Twenty-third Representative District, and be entitled to one representative.

The County of Iron shall constitute the Twenty-fourth Representative District, and be entitled to one representative.

The County of Washington shall constitute the Twenty-fifth Representative District, and be entitled to one representative.

The County of Kane shall constitute the Twenty-sixth Representative District, and be entitled to one representative.

The County of San Juan shall constitute the Twenty-seventh Representative District, and be entitled to one representative.

SENATORIAL DISTRICTS.

Until otherwise provided by law, the Senatorial Districts shall be constituted and numbered as follows:

The Counties of Box Elder and Tooele shall constitute the First District, and be entitled to one senator.

The County of Cache shall constitute the Second District, and be entitled to one senator.

The Counties of Rich, Morgan and Davis shall constitute the Third District, and be entitled to one senator.

The County of Weber shall constitute the Fourth District, and be entitled to two senators.

The Counties of Summit and Wasatch shall constitute the Fifth District, and be entitled to one senator.

The County of Salt Lake shall constitute the Sixth District, and be entitled to five senators.

The County of Utah shall constitute the Seventh District, and be entitled to two senators.

The Counties of Juab and Millard shall constitute the Eighth District, and be entitled to one senator.

The County of San Pete shall constitute the Ninth District, and be entitled to one senator.

The Counties of Sevier, Wayne, Piute, and Garfield shall constitute the Tenth District, and be entitled to one senator.

The Counties of Beaver, Iron, Washington and Kane shall constitute the Eleventh District, and be entitled to one senator.

The Counties of Emery, Carbon, Uintah, Grand, and San Juan shall constitute the Twelfth District, and be entitled to one senator.

ARTICLE X.

EDUCATION.

SECTION 1. The Legislature shall provide for the establishment and maintenance of a uniform system of public schools, which shall be open to all the children of the State, and free from sectarian control.

SEC. 2. The Public School System shall include kindergarten schools; common schools, consisting of primary and grammar grades; high schools; an Agricultural College; a University, and such other schools as the Legislature may establish. The common school shall be free. The other departments of the system shall be supported as provided by law: *Provided,* That high schools may be maintained free in all cities of the first and second class now constituting school districts, and in such other cities and districts as may be designated by the Legislature. But where the proportion of school moneys apportioned or accruing to any city or district shall not be sufficient to maintain all the free schools in such city or district, the high schools shall be supported by local taxation.

SEC. 3. The proceeds of all lands that have been, or may be granted by the United States to this State, for the support of the common schools; the proceeds of all property that may accrue to the State by escheat or forfeiture; and all unclaimed shares and dividends of any corporation incorporated under the laws of this State; the proceeds of the sale of timber, minerals or other property from school and State lands, other than those granted for specific purposes; and the five per centum of the net proceeds of the sales of public lands lying within the State, which shall be sold by the United States, subsequent to the admission of this State into the Union, shall be and remain a perpetual fund, to be called the State School Fund, the interest of which only, together with such other means as the Legislature may provide, shall be distributed among the several school districts according to the school population residing therein.

SEC. 4. The location and establishment by existing laws of the University of Utah, and Agricultural College are hereby confirmed, and all the rights, immunities, franchises and endowments heretofore granted or conferred, are hereby perpetuated unto said University and Agricultural College respectively.

SEC. 5. The proceeds of the sale of lands reserved by an Act of Congress, approved February 21st, 1855, for the establishment of the University of Utah, and of all the lands granted by an Act of Congress, approved July 16th, 1894, shall constitute permanent funds, to be safely invested and held by the State; and the income thereof shall be used exclusively for the support and maintenance of the different institutions and colleges, respectively, in accordance with the requirements and conditions of said acts of Congress.

SEC. 6. In cities of the first and second class, the public school system shall be maintained and controlled, by the Board of Education of such cities, separate and apart from the Counties in which said cities are located.

SEC. 7. All public School funds shall be guaranteed by the State against loss or diversion.

SEC. 8. The general control and supervision of the Public School System shall be vested in a State Board of Education, consisting of the Superintendent of Public Instruction, and such other persons as the Legislature may provide.

SEC. 9. Neither the Legislature nor the State Board of Education shall have power to prescribe text books to be used in the common schools.

SEC. 10. Institutions for the Deaf and Dumb, and for the Blind, are hereby established. All property belonging to the School for the Deaf and Dumb, heretofore connected with the University of Utah, shall be transferred to said Institution for the Deaf and Dumb. All the proceeds of the lands granted by the United States for the support of a Deaf and Dumb Asylum, and for an Institution for the Blind, shall be a perpetual fund for the maintenance of said Institutions. It shall be a trust fund, the principal of which shall remain inviolate, guaranteed by the State against loss or diversion.

SEC. 11. The Metric System shall be taught in the public schools of the State.

SEC. 12. Neither religious nor partisan test or qualification shall be required of any person as a condition of admission, as teacher or student, into any public educational institution of the State.

Sec. 13. Neither the Legislature nor any county, city, town, school district or other public corporation, shall make any appropriation to aid in the support of any school, seminary, academy, college, university or other institution, controlled in whole, or in part by any church, sect or denomination whatever.

ARTICLE XI.

COUNTIES, CITIES AND TOWNS.

Section 1. The several counties of the Territory of Utah, existing at the time of the adoption of this Constitution, are hereby recognized as legal subdivisions of this State, and the precincts and school districts now existing in the said counties, as legal subdivisions thereof, and they shall so continue until changed by law in pursuance of article.

Sec. 2. No County Seat shall be removed unless two-thirds of the qualified electors of the county, voting on the proposition at a general exection, shall vote in favor of such removal, and two-thirds of the votes cast on the proposition shall be required to re-locate a county seat. A proposition of removal shall not be submitted in the same county more than once in four years.

Sec. 3. No territory shall be stricken from any county unless a majority of the voters living in such territory, as well as of the county to which it is to· be annexed, shall vote therefor, and then only under such conditions as may be prescribed by general law.

Sec. 4. The Legislature shall establish a system of county government, which shall be uniform throughout the State, and by general laws shall provide for precinct and township organizations.

Sec. 5. Corporations for municipal purposes shall not be created by special laws, the Legislature, by general laws, shall provide for the incorporation, organization, and classification of cities and towns in proportion to population; which laws may be altered, amended or repealed.

Sec. 6. No municipal corportion, shall directly or in-directly, lease, sell, alien or dispose of any water-works, water-rights, or sources of water supply now, or hereafter to be owned or controlled by it, but all such water-works, water-rights and sources of water supply now owned or hereafter to be acquired by any municipal corporation, shall be preserved, maintained and operated by it for supplying its inhabitants with water at reasonable charges: *Provided,* That nothing herein contained shall be construed to prevent any such municipal corporation from exchanging water-rights, or sources of water supply, for other water-rights or sources of water supply of equal value, and to be devoted in like manner to the public supply of its inhabitants.

ARTICLE XII.

CORPORATIONS.

SECTION 1. Corporations may be formed under general laws, but shall not be created by special acts. All laws relating to corporations may be altered, amended or repealed by the Legislature, and all corporations doing business in this State, may, as to such business, be regulated, limited or restrained by law.

SEC. 2. All existing charters, franchises, special or exclusive privileges, under which an actual and bona fide organization shall not have taken place, and business been commenced in good faith, at the time of the adoption of this Constitution, shall thereafter have no validity; and no corporation in existence at the time of the adoption of this Constitution shall have the benefit of future legislation without first filing in the office of the Secretary of State, an acceptance of the provisions of this Constitution.

SEC. 3. The Legislature shall not extend any franchise or charter, nor remit the forfeiture of any franchise or charter of any corporation now existing, or which shall hereafter exist under the laws of this State.

SEC. 4. The term "Corporation," as used in this article, shall be construed to include all associations and joint stock companies having any powers or privileges of corporations not possessed by individuals or partnerships, and all corporations shall have the right to sue, and shall be subject to be sued, in all courts, in like cases as natural persons.

SEC. 5. Corporations shall not issue stock, except to bona fide subscribers thereof or their assignee, nor shall any corporation issue any bond, or other obligation, for the payment of money, except for money or property received, or labor done. The stock of corporations shall not be increased, except in pursuance of general law, nor shall any law authorize the increase of stock without the consent of the person or persons holding the larger amount in value of the stock, or without due notice of the proposed increase having previously been given in such manner as may be prescribed by law. All fictitious increase of stock or indebtedness shall be void.

SEC. 6. No corporations organized outside of this State, shall be allowed to transact business within the State, on conditions more favorable than those prescribed by law to similar corporations, organized under the laws of this State.

SEC. 7. No corporation shall lease or alienate any franchise, so as to relieve the franchise or property held thereunder from the liabilities of the lessor, or grantor, lessee, or grantee, contracted or incurred in operation, use or enjoyment of such franchise or any of its privileges.

SEC. 8. No law shall be passed granting the right to construct and operate a street railroad, telegraph, telephone or electric light plant within any city or incorporated town, without the consent of the local authorities who have the control of the street or highway proposed to be occupied for such purposes.

SEC. 9. No corporation shall do business in this State, without having one or more places of business, with an authorized agent or agents, upon whom process may be served; nor without first filing a certified copy of its articles of incorporation with the Secretary of State.

SEC. 10. No corporation shall engage in any business other than that expressly authorized in its charter, or articles of incorporation.

SEC. 11. The exercise of the right of eminent domain shall never be so abridged or construed, as to prevent the Legislature from taking the property and franchises of incorporated companies, and subjecting them to public use the same as the property of individuals.

Sec. 12. All railroad **and other** transportation companies are **declared** to be common carriers, **and** subject to legislative control; **and** such companies shall receive and transport each **other's** passengers and freight, without discrimination **or unnecessary delay.**

Sec. 13. No **railroad** corporation **shall** consolidate **its** stock, property or franchises with any other railroad corporation owning a competing **line.**

Sec. 14. The rolling stock, and other moveable property, belonging to any railroad **company or** corporation in this State, shall be considered personal property, **and** shall **be liable to** taxation and to execution and sale, in **the same manner as the** personal property of individuals, and such **property shall not be** exempted **from** execution and sale.

Sec. 15. The Legislature shall pass **laws establishing reasonable maximum** rates **of charges,** for **the transportation of** passengers **and** freight, **for** correcting abuses, and preventing discrimination and extortion **in** rates of freight **and** passenger tariffs by the different railroads, and other common carriers in **the** State, and shall enforce such laws by adequate penalties.

Sec. 16. No corporation or association shall bring any armed person or bodies of men into this State for the preservation of the peace, or the suppression of domestic troubles without authority of law.

Sec. 17. No officer, employee, attorney **or agent of any** corporation, company or association doing business under, or by virtue of any municipal charter or franchise, **shall be eligible to** or permitted to hold any municipal **office, in the** municipality granting such charter or franchise.

Sec. 18. The stockholders **in every** corporation, and joint **stock** association for **banking** purposes, **in** addition to the amount of **capital stock subscribed** and fully **paid** by them, shall be **individually** responsible **for an** additional amount, equal to the **amount of** their stock **in** such corporation, for all its debts and **liabilities** of every **kind.**

Sec. 19. Every person in this State shall be free to obtain employment whenever possible, and any person, corporation, or agent, servant **or** employee thereof, maliciously interfering or hindering **in** any way, any person from obtaining, or enjoying employment already obtained, from any other corporation or person, shall be deemed guilty of a crime. The Legislature shall provide by law for the enforcement of this section.

SEC. 20. Any combination by individuals, corporations, or associations, having for its object or effect the controlling of the price of any products of the soil, or of any article of manufacture or commerce, or the cost of exchange or transportation, is prohibited, and hereby declared unlawful, and against public policy. The Legislature shall pass laws for the enforcement of this section by adequate penalties, and in case of incorporated companies, if necessary may declare a forfeiture of their franchise.

ARTICLE XIII.

REVENUE AND TAXATION.

SECTION 1. The fiscal year shall begin on the first day of January, unless changed by the Legislature.

SEC. 2. All property in the State, not exempt under the laws of the United States, or under this Constitution, shall be taxed in proportion to its value, to be ascertained as provided by law. The word property, as used in this article, is hereby declared to include moneys, credits, bonds, stocks, franchises and all matters and things (real, personal and mixed) capable of private ownership; but this shall not be so construed as to authorize the taxation of the stocks of any company or corporation, when the property of such company or corporation represented by such stocks, has been taxed. The Legislature shall provide by law for an annual tax sufficient, with other sources of revenue, to defray the estimated ordinary expenses of the State for each fiscal year. For the purpose of paying the State debt, if any there be, the Legislature shall provide for levying a tax annually, sufficient to pay the annual interest, and principal of such debt, within twenty years from the final passage of the law creating the debt.

SEC. 3. The Legislature shall provide by law a uniform and equal rate of assessment and taxation on all property in the State, according to its value in money, and shall prescribe by general law such regulations as shall secure a just valuation for taxation of all property; so that every person and corpora-

tion shall **pay** a tax in proportion to **the value** of his, her or its
property: *Provided,* That a deduction of debits from credits
may be authorized: *Provided further,* That the property of the
United States, of the State, counties, cities, towns, school districts,
municipal corporations **and** public libraries, **lots** with the **build-**
ings thereon used exclusively for either religious worship **or**
charitable purposes, and **places** of burial not held or **used for**
private or corporate **benefit, shall be exempt** from taxation.
Ditches, **canals,** and flumes **owned and used by** individuals **or**
corporations **for** irrigating **lands owned by such individuals or**
corporations, or the individual members thereof, **shall not be**
separately **taxed** so long **as they shall be owned and used exclu-**
sively for **such** purpose.

Sec. 4. All mines and mining claims, both placer and rock
in place, containing or bearing gold, silver, copper, lead, coal or
other valuable mineral deposits, after purchase thereof from the
United States, shall be taxed at the price paid the United States
therefor, unless the surface ground, or some part thereof, of
such mine or claim, is used for other than mining purposes, and
has a separate and independent value for such other purposes;
in which case said surface ground, or any part thereof, so used
for other than mining purposes, shall be taxed at its value for
such other purposes, as provided by law; and all the machinery
used in mining, and all property and surface improvements
upon or appurtenant to mines and mining claims, which have a
value separate and independent of such mines or mining claims,
and the net annual proceeds of all mines and mining claims,
shall be taxed as provided by law.

Sec. 5. The Legislature shall not impose taxes for the
purpose of any county, city, town or other municipal corporation, but may, by law vest, in the corporate authorities thereof,
respectively, the power to assess and collect taxes for all purposes of such corporation.

Sec. 6. An accurate statement of the receipts and expenditures of the public moneys, shall be published annually in
such manner as the Legislature may provide.

Sec. 7. The rate of taxation on property, for State purposes, shall never exceed eight mills on each dollar of valuation;
and whenever the taxable property within the State shall amount
to two hundred million dollars, the rate shall not exceed five

mills on each dollar of valuation; and whenever the taxable property within the State shall amount to three hundred million dollars, the rate shall never thereafter exceed four mills on each dollar of valuation; unless a proposition to increase such rate, specifying the rate proposed, and the time during which the same shall be levied, be first submitted to a vote of such of the qualified electors of the State as, in the year next preceding such election, shall have paid a property tax assessed to them within the State, and the majority of those voting thereon shall vote in favor thereof, in such manner as may be provided by law.

SEC. 8. The making of profit out of public moneys, or using the same for any purpose not authorized by law, by any public officer, shall be deemed a felony, and shall be punished as provided by law, but part of such punishment shall be disqualification to hold public office.

SEC. 9. No appropriation shall be made, or any expenditure authorized by the Legislature, whereby the expenditure of the State, during any fiscal year, shall exceed the total tax then provided for by law, and applicable for such appropriation or expenditure, unless the Legislature making such appropriation, shall provide for levying a sufficient tax, not exceeding the rates allowed in section seven of this article, to pay such appropriation or expenditure within such fiscal year. This provision shall not apply to appropriations or expenditures to suppress insurrections, defend the State, or assist in defending the United States in time of war.

SEC. 10. All corporations or persons in this State, or doing business herein, shall be subject to taxation for State, county, school, municipal or other purposes, on the real and personal property owned or used by them within the Territorial limits of the authority levying the tax.

SEC. 11. Until otherwise provided by law, there shall be a State Board of Equalization, consisting of the Governor, State Auditor, State Treasurer, Secretary of State and Attorney-General; also, in each county of this State, a County Board of Equalization, consisting of the Board of County Commissioners of said county. The duty of the State Board of Equalization shall be to adjust and equalize the valuation of the real and personal property among the several counties of the State.

The duty of the County Board of Equalization shall be to adjust and equalize the valuation of the real and personal property within their respective counties. Each Board shall also perform such other duties as may be prescribed by law.

SEC. 12. Nothing in this Constitution shall be construed to prevent the Legislature from providing a stamp tax, or a tax based on income, occupation, licenses, franchises or mortgages.

ARTICLE XIV.

PUBLIC DEBT.

SECTION 1. To meet casual deficits or failures in revenue, and for necessary expenditures for public purposes, including the erection of public buildings, and for the payment of all Territorial indebtedness assumed by the State, the State may contract debts, not exceeding in the aggregate at any one time, the sum of two hundred thousand dollars over and above the amount of the Territorial indebtedness assumed by the State. But when the said Territorial indebtedness shall have been paid, the State shall never contract any indebtedness, except as in the next section provided, in excess of the sum of two hundred thousand dollars, and all moneys arising from loans herein authorized, shall be applied solely to the purposes for which they were obtained.

SEC. 2. The State may contract debts to repel invasion, suppress insurrection, or to defend the State in war, but the money arising from the contracting of such debts shall be applied solely to the purpose for which it was obtained.

SEC. 3. No debt in excess of the taxes for the current year shall be created by any county or subdivision thereof, or by any school district therein, or by any city, town or village, or any subdivision thereof in this State; unless the proposition to create such debt, shall have been submitted to a vote of such qualified electors as shall have paid a property tax therein, in the year preceding such election, and a majority of those voting thereon shall have voted in favor of incurring such debt.

SEC. 4. When authorized to create indebtedness as provided in Section three of this Article, no county shall become indebted to an amount, including existing indebtedness, exceeding two per centum. No city, town, school district or other municipal corporation, shall become indebted to an amount, including existing indebtedness, exceeding four per centum of the value of the taxable property therein, the value to be ascertained by the last assessment for State and county purposes, previous to the incurring of such indebtedness; except that in incorporated cities the assessment shall be taken from the last assessment for city purposes: *Provided*, That no part of the indebtedness allowed in this section, shall be incurred for other than strictly county, city, town or school district purposes: *Provided, further*, That any city or town when authorized as provided in section three of this article, may be allowed to incur a larger indebtedness, not exceeding four per centum additional, for supplying such city or town with water, artificial light or sewers, when the works for supplying such water, light and sewers, shall be owned and controlled by the municipality.

SEC. 5. All moneys borrowed by or on behalf of the State, or any legal subdivision thereof, shall be used solely for the purpose specified in the law authorizing the loan.

SEC. 6. The State shall not assume the debt, or any part thereof, of any county, city, town or school district.

SEC. 7. Nothing in this article shall be so construed as to impair or add to the obligation of any debt heretofore contracted, in accordance with the laws of Utah Territory, by any county, city, town or school district, or to prevent the contracting of any debt, or the issuing of bonds therefor, in accordance with said laws, upon any proposition for that purpose, which, according to said laws, may have been submitted to a vote of the qualified electors of any county, city, town or school district before the day on which this Constitution takes effect.

ARTICLE XV.

MILITIA.

SECTION 1. The militia shall consist of all able-bodied male inhabitants of the State between the ages of eighteen and forty-five years, except such as are exempt by law.

SEC. 2. The Legislature shall provide by law for the organization, equipment and discipline of the militia, which shall conform as nearly as practicable to the regulations for the government of the armies of the United States.

ARTICLE XVI.

LABOR.

SECTION 1. The rights of labor shall have just protection through laws calculated to promote the industrial welfare of the State.

SEC. 2. The Legislature shall provide by law, for a Board of Labor, Conciliation and Arbitration, which shall fairly represent the interests of both capital and labor. The Board shall perform duties, and receive compensation as prescribed by law

SEC. 3. The Legislature shall prohibit:

First. The employment of women, or of children under the age of fourteen years, in underground mines.

Second. The contracting of convict labor.

Third. The labor of convicts outside prison grounds, except on public works under the direct control of the State.

Fourth. The political and commercial control of employees.

SEC. 4. The exchange of black lists by railroad companies or other corporations, associations or persons is prohibited.

SEC. 5. The right of action to recover damages for injuries resulting in death, shall never be abrogated, and the amount recoverable shall not be subject to any statutory limitation.

SEC. 6. Eight hours shall constitue a day's work on all works or undertakings carried on or aided by the State, county or municipal governments ; and the Legislature shall pass laws to provide for the health and safety of employees in factories, smelters and mines.

SEC. 7. The Legislature, by appropriate legislation, shall provide for the enforcement of the provisions of this article.

ARTICLE XVII.

WATER RIGHTS.

SECTION 1. All existing rights to the use of any of the waters in this State for any useful or beneficial purpose, are hereby recognized and confirmed.

ARTICLE XVIII.

FORESTRY.

SECTION 1. The Legislature shall enact laws to prevent the destruction of and to preserve the forests on the lands of the State, and upon any part of the public domain, the control of which may be conferred by Congress upon the State.

ARTICLE XIX.

PUBLIC BUILDINGS AND STATE INSTITUTIONS.

SECTION 1. All institutions and other property of the Territory, upon the adoption of this Constitution, shall become the institutions and property of the State of Utah.

SEC. 2. Reformatory and penal institutions, and those for the benefit of the insane, blind, deaf and dumb, and such other institutions as the public good may require, shall be established and supported by the State in such manner, and under such boards of control as may be prescribed by law.

SEC. 3. The Public Institutions of the State are hereby permanently located at the places hereinafter named, each to have the lands specifically granted to it by the United States, in the Act of Congress, approved July 16th, 1894, to be disposed of and used in such manner as the Legislature may provide:

First. The Seat of Government, and the State Fair at Salt Lake City, and the State Prison in the County of Salt Lake.

Second. The Institutions for the Deaf and Dumb, and the Blind, and the State Reform School at Ogden City, in the County of Weber.

Third. The State Insane Asylum at Provo City, in the County of Utah.

ARTICLE XX.

PUBLIC LANDS.

SECTION 1. All lands of the State that have been, or may hereafter be granted to the State by Congress, and all lands acquired by gift, grant or devise, from any person or corporation, or that may otherwise be acquired, are hereby accepted, and declared to be the public lands of the State; and shall be held in trust for the people, to be disposed of as may be provided by law, for the respective purposes for which they have been or may be granted, donated, devised or otherwise acquired.

ARTICLE XXI.

SALARIES.

SECTION 1. All State, district, city, county, town and school officers, excepting notaries public, boards of arbitration, court commissioners, justices of the peace and constables, shall be paid fixed and definite salaries: *Provided,* That city justices may be paid by salary when so determined by the mayor and council of such cities.

SEC. 2. The Legislature shall provide by law, the fees which shall be collected by all officers within the State. Notaries public, boards of arbitration, court commissioners, justices of the peace, and constables paid by fees, shall accept said fees as their full compensation. But all other State, district, county, city, town and school officers, shall be required by law to keep a true and correct account of all fees collected by them, and to pay the same into the proper treasury, and the officer whose duty it is to collect such fees shall be held responsible under his bond for the same.

ARTICLE XXII.

MISCELLANEOUS.

SECTION 1. The Legislature shall provide by law, for the selection by each head of a family, an exemption of a homestead, which may consist of one or more parcels of land, together with the appurtenances and improvements thereon, of the value of at least fifteen hundred dollars, from sale on execution.

SEC. 2. Real and personal estate of every female, acquired before marriage; and all property to which she may afterwards become entitled by purchase, gift, grant, inheritance or devise, shall be and remain the estate and property of such female, and shall not be liable for the debts, obligations or engagements of her husband, and may be conveyed, devised or bequeathed by her as if she were unmarried.

ARTICLE XXIII.

AMENDMENTS.

SECTION 1. Any amendment or amendments to this Constitution may be proposed in either house of the Legislature, and if two-thirds of all the members elected to each of the two houses, shall vote in favor thereof, such proposed amendment or amendments shall be entered on their respective journals with the yeas and nays taken thereon; and the Legislature shall cause the same to be published in at least one newspaper in every county of the State, where a newspaper is published, for two months immediately preceding the next general election, at which time the said amendment or amendments shall be submitted to the electors of the State, for their approval or rejection, and if a majority of the electors voting thereon shall approve the same, such amendment or amendments shall become part of this Constitution. If two or more amendments are proposed, they shall be so submitted as to enable the electors to vote on each of them separately.

SEC. 2. Whenever two-thirds of the members, elected to each branch of the Legislature, shall deem it necessary to call a convention to revise or amend this Constitution, they shall recommend to the electors to vote at the next general election for or against a convention, and, if a majority of all the electors, voting at such election, shall vote for a convention, the Legislature, at its next session, shall provide by law for calling the same. The convention shall consist of not less than the number of members in both branches of the Legislature.

SEC. 3. No Constitution or amendments adopted by such convention, shall have validity until submitted to and adopted by a majority of the electors of the State voting at the next general election.

ARTICLE XXIV.

SCHEDULE.

SECTION 1. In order that no inconvenience may arise, by reason of the change from a Territorial to a State government, it is hereby declared that all writs, actions, prosecutions, judgments, claims and contracts, as well of individuals as of bodies corporate, both public and private, shall continue as if no change had taken place; and all process which may issue, under the authority of the Territory of Utah, previous to its admission into the Union, shall be as valid as if issued in the name of the State of Utah.

SEC. 2. All laws of the Territory of Utah now in force, not repugnant to this Constitution, shall remain in force until they expire by their own limitations, or are altered or repealed by the Legislature. The act of the Governor and Legislative Assembly of the Territory of Utah, entitled, "An Act to punish polygamy and other kindred offenses," approved February 4th, A. D. 1892, in so far as the same defines and imposes penalties for polygamy, is hereby declared to be in force in the State of Utah.

SEC. 3. Any persons, who, at the time of the admission of the State into the Union, may be confined under lawful commitments, or otherwise lawfully held to answer for alleged violations of any of the criminal laws of the Territory of Utah, shall continue to be so held or confined, until discharged therefrom by the proper courts of the State.

SEC. 4. All fines, penalties and forfeitures accruing to the Territory of Utah, or to the people of the United States in the Territory of Utah, shall inure to this State, and all debts, liabilities and obligations of said Territory, shall be valid against the State, and enforced as may be provided by law.

SEC. 5. All recognizances heretofore taken, or which may be taken before the change from a Territorial to a State government, shall remain valid, and shall pass to and be prosecuted in the name of the State; and all bonds executed to the Governor of the Territory, or to any other officer or court in his or their official capacity, or to any official board for the benefit of the Territory of Utah, or the people thereof, shall pass to the Governor or other officer, court or board, and his or their successors in office, for the uses therein, respectively expressed, and may be sued on, and recovered, accordingly. Assessed taxes and all revenue, property, real, personal or mixed, and all judgments, bonds, specialties, choses in action, claims and debts, of whatsoever description; and all records and public archives of the Territory of Utah, shall issue and vest in the State of Utah, and may be sued for and recoveced, in the same manner, and to the same extent by the State of Utah, as the same could have been by the Territory of Utah; and all fines, taxes, penalties and forfeitures, due or owing to any county, municipality or school district therein, at the time the State shall be admitted into the Union, are hereby respectively assigned and transferred, and the same shall be payable to the county, municipality or school district, as the case may be, and payment thereof be enforced under the laws of the State.

SEC. 6. All criminal prosecutions, and penal actions, which may have arisen, or which may arise before the change from a Territorial to a State Government, and which shall then be pending, shall be prosecuted to judgment and execution in the name of the State, and in the court having jurisdiction thereof. All offenses committed against the laws of the Territory of Utah, before the change from a Territorial to a State government, and which shall not have been prosecuted before such change, may be prosecuted in the name, and by the authority of the State of Utah, with like effect as though such change had not taken place, and all penalties incurred shall remain the same, as if this Constitution had not been adopted.

SEC. 7. All actions, cases, proceedings and matters, pending in the Supreme and District Courts of the Territory of Utah, at the time the State shall be admitted into the Union, and all files, records and indictments relating thereto, except as otherwise provided herein, shall be appropriately transferred to the Supreme and District Courts of the State respectively; and thereafter all such actions, matters and cases, shall be proceeded with in the proper State courts. All actions, cases, proceedings and matters which shall be pending in the District Courts of the Territory of Utah, at the time of the admission of the State into the Union, whereof the United States Circuit or District Courts might have had jurisdiction had there been a State government at the time of the commencement thereof respectively, shall be transferred to the proper United States Circuit and District Courts respectively; and all files, records, indictments and proceedings relating thereto, shall be transferred to said United States Courts: *Provided*, That no civil actions, other than causes and proceedings of which the said United States courts shall have exclusive jurisdiction, shall be transferred to either of said United States Courts except upon **motion or** petition by one of the parties thereto, made **under and** in accordance with the act or acts of the Congress of **the** United States, and **such** motion and petition not being **made, all such** cases shall be proceeded with in the **proper State courts.**

Sec. 8. **Upon** a **change from** Territorial to State government, the **seal in use** by the Supreme Court **of** the Territory **of** Utah, until otherwise **provided** by law, **shall pass to** and be**come** the **seal of** the **Supreme** Court of the **State,** and the several District Courts of **the** State may adopt seals for their respective courts, until otherwise provided by law.

Sec. 9. **When** the **State is** admitted into the Union, and **the** District Courts in the respective districts are organized, the **books, records,** papers and proceedings of the probate court in **each county,** and all causes **and** matters of administration pending therein, upon the expiration of the term of office of the Probate Judge, **on** the second **Monday** in January, 1896, shall pass **into** the jurisdiction **and** possession of the District Court, which shall proceed **to** final judgment or decree, **order or** other determination in the several **matters** and causes, as the Territorial Probate Court might have **done, if** this Constitution had **not been** adopted. And until **the** expiration of the term of office **of the** Probate Judges, such Probate Judges shall perform the **duties now** imposed upon them by the laws of the Territory. The District Court shall have appellate **and** revisory jurisdiction over **the** decisions **of** the Probate Courts, **as now provided by** law, until such latter **courts** expire by limitation.

Sec. 10. All officers, **civil** and military, now holding their offices and appointments **in this** Territory by authority of law, shall continue **to** hold **and exercise** their respective offices and appointments, until superceded **under this** Constitution: *Provided,* That **the** provisions **of this** section shall be subject to **the** provisions of the **Act of** Congress, providing for the admission **of** the State of Utah, approved by the President of **the United States** on July 16th, 1894.

Sec. **11.** The election for the adoption or rejection of this Constitution, and for State **officers** herein provided for, shall be held on **the** Tuesday next after **the** first Monday in November, 1895, **and** shall be conducted according to the laws of the Territory **and** the provisions of the Enabling Act; the votes cast at said election shall be canvassed, and returns made, in the same manner as was provided for in the election for delegates to the Constitutional Convention.

Provided, That all male citizens of the United States, over the age of twenty-one years, who have resided in the Territory for one year prior to such election, are hereby authorized to vote for or against the adoption of this Constitution, and for the State Officers herein provided for. The returns of said election shall be made to the Utah Commission, who shall cause the same to be canvassed, and shall certify the result of the vote for or against the Constitution, to the President of the United States, in the manner required by the Enabling Act; and said Commission shall issue certificates of election to the persons elected to said offices severally, and shall make and file with the Secretary of the Territory, an abstract, certified to by them, of the number of votes cast for each person for each of said offices, and of the total number of votes cast in each county.

SEC. 12. The State officers to be voted for at the time of the adoption of this Constitution, shall be a Governor, Secretary of State, State Auditor, State Treasurer, Attorney General, Superintendent of Public Instruction, members of the Senate and House of Representatives, three Supreme Judges, nine District Judges, and a Representative to Congress.

SEC. 13. In case of a contest of election between candidates, at the first general election under this Constitution, for Judges of the District Courts, the evidence shall be taken in the manner prescribed by the Territorial laws, and the testimony so taken shall be certified to the Secretary of State, and said officer, together with the Governor and the Treasurer of the State, shall review the evidence, and determine who is entitled to the certificate of election.

SEC. 14. This Constitution shall be submitted for adoption or rejection, to a vote of the qualified electors of the proposed State, at the general election to be held on the Tuesday next after the first Monday in November, A. D. 1895. At the said election the ballot shall be in the following form:

For the Constitution. Yes. No.

As a heading to each of said ballots there shall be printed on each ballot the following Instructions to Voters:

All persons desiring to vote for the Constitution must erase the word " No."

All persons desiring to vote against the Constitution must erase the word " Yes."

Sec. 15. The Legislature, at its first session, shall provide for the election of all officers, whose election is not provided for elsewhere in this Constitution, and fix the time for the commencement and durations of their terms.

Sec. 16. The provisions of this Constitution shall be in force from the day on which the President of the United States shall issue his proclamation, declaring the State of Utah admitted into the Union; and the terms of all officers elected at the first election under the provisions of this Constitution, shall commence on the first Monday, next succeeding the issue of said proclamation. Their terms of office shall expire when their successors are elected and qualified under this Constitution.

Done in Convention at Salt Lake City, in the Territory of Utah, this eighth day of May, in the year of our Lord one thousand eight hundred and ninety-five, and of the Independence of the United States the one hundred and nineteenth.

JOHN HENRY SMITH,
President.

Attest:

PARLEY P. CHRISTENSEN,
Secretary.

LOUIS BERNHARDT ADAMS,
RUFUS ALBERN ALLEN,
ANDREW SMITH ANDERSON,
JOHN RICHARD BARNES,
JOHN RUTLEDGE BOWDLE,
JOHN SELL BOYER,
THEODORE BRANDLEY,
HERBERT GUION BUTTON,
WILLIAM BUYS,
CHESTER CALL,
GEORGE MOUSLEY CANNON,
JOHN FOY CHIDESTER,
PARLEY CHRISTIANSEN,
THOMAS H. CLARK, JR.,

LOUIS LAVILLE CORAY,
ELMER ELLSWORTH CORFMAN,
CHARLES CRANE,
WILLIAM CREER,
GEORGE CUNNINGHAM,
ARTHUR JOHN CUSHING,
WILLIAM DRIVER,
DENNIS CLAY EICHNOR,
ALMA ELDREDGE,
GEORGE RHODES EMERY,
ANDREAS ENGBERG,
DAVID EVANS,
ABEL JOHN EVANS,
LORIN FARR,

Samuel Francis,
William Henry Gibbs,
Charles Carrol Goodwin,
James Frederic Green,
Francis Asbury Hammond,
Charles Henry Hart,
Harry Haynes,
John Daniel Holladay,
Robert W. Heyborne,
Samuel Hood Hill,
William Howard,
Henry Hughes,
Joseph Alonzo Hyde,
Anthony Woodward Ivins,
Wm. F. James,
Lycurgus Johnson,
Joseph Loftis Jolley,
Frederick John Kiesel,
Daniel Keith,
Thomas Kearns,
William Jasper Kerr,
Andrew Kimball,
James Nathaniel Kimball,
Richard G. Lambert,
Lauritz Larsen,
Christen Peter Larsen,
Hyrum Lemmon,
Theodore Belden Lewis,
William Lowe,
Peter Lowe,
James Paton Low,
Anthony Canute Lund,
Karl G. Maeser,
Richard Mackintosh,
Thomas Maloney,
William H. Maughn,
Robert McFarland,
Geo. P. Miller,
Elias Morris,
Jacob Moritz,

John Riggs Murdock,
Joseph Royal Murdock,
James David Murdock,
Aquilla Nebeker,
Jeremiah Day Page,
Edward Partridge,
J. D. Peters,
Mons Peterson,
James Christian Peterson,
Franklin Pierce,
Wm. B. Preston,
Alonzo Hazelton Raleigh,
Franklin Snyder Richards,
Joel Ricks,
Brigham Henry Roberts,
Jasper Robertson,
Joseph Eldridge Robinson,
Willis Eugene Robison,
George Ryan,
John Henry Smith,
George B. Squires,
William Gilson Sharp,
Harrison Tuttle Shurtliff,
Edmund Hunter Snow,
Hyrum Hupp Spencer,
David Brainerd Stover,
Charles Nettleton Strevell,
Charles William Symons,
Daniel Thompson,
Moses Thatcher,
Ingwald Conrad Thoresen,
Joseph Ephraim Thorne,
Samuel R. Thurman,
William Grant Van Horne,
Charles Stetson Varian,
Heber M. Wells,
Noble Warrum, Jr.,
Orson Ferguson Whitney,
Joseph John Williams.